THE BLUE TEAPOT

Sandy Cove Stories

By ALICE DALGLIESH

Illustrated by Hildegard Woodward

Miss Letty lived all alone with Thomas, the black cat. She was never lonely until one day she bought a lovely blue teapot with cups and saucers to match. The next morning she went to the Orphans' Home where she found two little girls whom she named Sara and Abigail. The title story tells their adventures together, keeping house with Miss Letty and Thomas.

The background of these adventures is Sandy Cove, a real village in Nova Scotia. The tales go on to tell of other characters in that delightful spot. There is an amusing story of Miranda and her seven white cats, of Zebedee who wanted to become a fisherman, Mary Lee and the lights of her Christmas tree, and others.

These tales are told with a delightful mixture of solemnity and humor that children love. Miss Dalgliesh has written successful books for the pre-school age. She is well known for her interesting work at Teachers' College of Columbia.

$2.75

The New York *Times* says of The Blue Teapot—"A delightful little book that deals with the simple things that little children enjoy in a thoroughly satisfactory way. There is plenty of incident, all well within a child's range of interest, and something of the freshness and charm of the blue water and green firs of Nova Scotia have found their way into the pages."

Parents Magazine says — "These stories have a direct appeal, with an irresistible charm and humor in the telling. A real feeling of sympathy in each of the tales. The pictures are attractive and have the literal touch which children enjoy."

Here is one of the little girls in the village of Sandy Cove, who figures in so many of this author's stories. She is holding "Relief's Rocker."

THE BLUE TEAPOT

SANDY COVE STORIES

By Alice Dalgliesh

The Little Wooden Farmer
A pre-school story to listen to and to play; with it is printed "The Jungle Pool."

The Choosing Book
A picture book game for small children.

The Blue Teapot
Stories of Sandy Cove, for boys and girls who have learned to read.

Relief's Rocker
A new story of Sandy Cove.

THE
BLUE TEAPOT

SANDY COVE STORIES

BY ALICE DALGLIESH

ILLUSTRATED BY HILDEGARD WOODWARD

New York
THE MACMILLAN COMPANY
1956

COPYRIGHT, 1931,
By THE MACMILLAN COMPANY

All rights reserved—no part of this book may be reproduced in any form without permission in writing from the publisher.

Set up and electrotyped.
Published, September, 1931.
Eighteenth Printing, 1956

PRINTED IN THE UNITED STATES OF AMERICA

TO MY FRIENDS
ON THE ROAD
TO FUNDY

CONTENTS

	PAGE
ABOUT SANDY COVE	1
THE BLUE TEAPOT	5
THE SEVEN WHITE CATS	27
THE GOLDEN WEDDING	41
ZEBEDEE, FISHERMAN	53
WHITE CHRISTMAS	63

ILLUSTRATIONS

	PAGE
Sara and Abigail at the edge of the bluff, overlooking the sea	15
Abigail was especially interested in cooking	17
Map of the cats from Sandy Cove to Tiverton	33
Great-grandmother and great-grandfather sat under an arch of tansy and golden rod	48
There they saw the lighted Christmas tree	71

THE BLUE TEAPOT
SANDY COVE STORIES

ABOUT SANDY COVE

These are stories from a village by the Bay of Fundy, where there are little white houses with gray roofs

—where hollyhocks grow as tall as houses

—and geraniums grow as tall as children

—where the trees are evergreens, dark green spruce, and sweet-smelling balsam, and no one needs to *buy* a Christmas tree.

There is sea on each side of the village. On one side is the Cove which leads out into Saint Mary's Bay, on the other side is the Bay of Fundy. You can find the Cove, and the big bay and the little bay, and all the places in the stories, on the map the artist has made for the end-papers of this book.

THE BLUE TEAPOT

THE BLUE TEAPOT

There was once a nice old lady whose name was Miss Letitia Brown. She was so kind and friendly that no one ever thought of calling her Miss Brown or even Miss Letitia. Everyone called her Miss Letty.

Miss Letty lived all by herself in a cottage at the top of a hill, overlooking the sea. It was a white cottage with a green door, a roof of weathered gray shingles, and a cheerful brick chimney from which there rose a curl of white smoke. All around the house were flowers and dark green fir trees.

Sometimes people asked Miss Letty if she did not feel lonely living all by herself in the little cottage.

"Lonely?" said Miss Letty. "Why should I be? I have Thomas, my big black cat, I have my flowers, and I can watch the fishing boats as they go and come. Why should I be lonely?"

Miss Letty's father had been a sea captain, and so Miss Letty loved the sea. Winter and summer she liked to sit at her window and look out across the blue waters of the Bay of Fundy. She could see the wharf and the beach. There at low tide the fishing boats lay stranded, looking awkward and ridiculous, while at high tide they floated proudly on the water.

Next to the sea, Miss Letty loved her garden. It was quite the loveliest garden in the village of Sandy Cove. On the sloping ground at the back of the house grew every flower you can possibly imagine. There was a border of lavender and white alyssum. Miss Letty planted that because it smelled so sweet on summer evenings. There was mignonette, there was snapdragon, white, yellow, and pink, and there was tall blue larkspur. Cosmos and dahlias grew against the fence.

Almost every time anyone passed by Miss Letty's house, she was in the garden, planting, weeding, watering. Or she would be coming down the path, with her arms full of flowers, and with Thomas, very dignified, waving his tail as he walked before her.

The only time that Miss Letty could not be seen in the garden was in the winter, when the snow lay thick on the ground and the wind sighed and moaned through the fir trees. Then Miss Letty sat snugly indoors by the fire and Thomas sat on the hearth rug, purring cozily and contentedly as the flames danced and the logs crackled.

Now for a long time Miss Letty was very happy. Then, one bright spring day when the fir trees were wearing their new green tips and the roads were bordered with violets and columbine, Miss Letty went down the hill to the village. She carried a basket on her arm, for she was going to the village store to buy tea and sugar and bacon.

Before she went into the store Miss Letty stopped to look in the window. Usually the window was not very interesting, for it held only the kettle that had been there for three years, some mixing bowls, and a few dusty plates. To-day it was different. The storekeeper must have felt it was spring, for the window was clean and the wares in it were neatly arranged. The kettle was still there, it is true, and so were the plates and the mixing bowls, but in the middle of the window was

A BLUE TEAPOT.

It was as blue as larkspur, as blue as the water of the Bay of Fundy, as blue as Miss Letty's Sunday dress. There were also four blue cups and saucers, four blue plates, and a blue sugar bowl and cream pitcher.

"I must have that teapot," said Miss Letty, walking into the store very quickly so that she would not have time to change her mind. In a very short time she came out with the blue teapot, the plates, the cups and saucers, and the pitcher and sugar bowl, all neatly packed in her basket. There was no sugar in the basket, nor was there any bacon. Miss Letty had forgotten those, though she had remembered the tea.

At suppertime Miss Letty put a white cloth on her little square table and set it very neatly with one blue plate, one blue cup, the cream pitcher and the empty sugar bowl. She made herself a cup of tea, cooked herself a piece of finnan haddie, and sat down to enjoy her supper. Somehow she did not enjoy it at all.

"There should be more blue cups and plates on this table," said Miss Letty. "Thomas, I believe that, after all, we are lonely."

Thomas tucked his paws under him and purred cozily.

"Yes, Thomas," said Miss Letty, "we are lonely. To-morrow we are going to find someone to live with us."

Thomas yawned, a wide pink yawn. He was tired of waiting for his share of finnan haddie.

The next morning, before Miss Letty had time to change her mind, she set out for the Orphans' Home, which was not very far from the village.

"I think I shall get a good, strong, plain girl of about fourteen," said Miss Letty to herself. "Then she can help me with the work and she will be most useful **in the garden.**"

But, as Miss Letty **went** in the gate of the Orphans' Home, she saw two little girls **standing under** an apple tree. They were about seven years old, they had pink cheeks and blue eyes, and—best of all—they had braids of long yellow hair.

It was quite too much for Miss Letty.

"Oh!" she said. "O-oh! Are you by any chance orphans and do you want to be adopted?"

"We would love to be adopted," said the two little girls, together. "No one has taken us because everyone seems to want one little girl with curls. We haven't curls and we are twins."

"I have always liked twins," said Miss Letty. "What are your names, my dears?"

"Dorothea," answered one twin.

"Dorinda," answered the other.

"Well," said Miss Letty, firmly, "I don't believe in fancy names, and I shall call you Sara and Abigail."

"We like those names as well as our own," said the twins, politely.

The long and the short of it was that when Miss Letty left the Orphans' Home she had promised to adopt the two little girls, but she asked for a week to get the house ready for them. As for the strong, plain, fourteen-year-old girl to help with the work, Miss Letty had forgotten all about her. She had a most remarkable way of forgetting things that did not seem particularly important.

"Twins!" said Miss Letty as she walked home feeling quite dazed but very happy. "Twins—seven years old—yellow hair—blue eyes—Sara—Abigail—what will Thomas think!"

The week that followed was the busiest one of Miss Letty's life. From morning till night she washed and scrubbed and ironed and arranged things. She spent a great deal of time getting a room

[11]

ready for the two little girls. From the old chest in the closet under the stairs she unearthed the most surprising and interesting things. After a good deal of thought she selected two patchwork quilts made by her mother, and a braided rug made by her grandmother. Fortunately there were already two beds in the room; indeed, as Miss Letty thought, the room seemed to have been planned for two little girls and to have stood waiting for them all these years.

"Thomas," said Miss Letty as she ironed the white frilly curtains, "Thomas, isn't it strange that all these years we did not know that we were lonely?" Thomas arched his back and rubbed against her legs.

At last the great day came and Miss Letty brought Abigail and Sara to their new home. It was a lovely, sunshiny afternoon as they walked up the fir-bordered road and turned in at Miss Letty's gate. The daffodils along the garden path danced in the breeze, a homelike curl of white smoke came from the chimney, and Thomas sat on the doorstep to welcome them.

"Oh, Miss Letty," said Abigail, "what a lovely place to live!"

"Oh, Miss Letty," said Sara, "is this dear little house really ours?"

Inside the house there were a great many *ah's!* and *oh's!* The blue tea set did not make Miss Letty feel at all lonely that night, for she could use three cups and three plates, in fact she used four because she even set a place for Thomas.

At eight o'clock, quite worn out with excitement, the little girls went to bed. Miss Letty went in quietly when she thought they were asleep. There was Abigail fast asleep under the blue and white patchwork quilt, and there was Sara fast asleep under the lavender and white patchwork quilt.

"I am not going to keep puzzling over which of these twins is which," said Miss Letty. "Most of the time I shall dress Abigail in blue or pink, and Sara in lavender or yellow. On Sundays they can dress alike. I think I shall be able to tell them apart, anyway, for Abigail's eyes are just a trifle bluer than Sara's, and Sara's hair is a trifle yellower than Abigail's."

Miss Letty and the twins had such good times together. They were polite and amiable little girls. When the minister came to call they put on their best pink dresses, they curtsied when he spoke to them, and Abigail handed him a cup of tea, while Sara brought in a little tray with cream and sugar. Miss Letty was very proud of them.

On summer evenings Miss Letty and the twins often had tea in the garden. They took out the small square table, the white tablecloth with the blue border, and, of course, the blue tea set. Miss Letty poured tea from the blue teapot, and Abigail and Sara took bites of Miss Letty's crisp, brown, crunchy cookies and thought what very lucky little girls they were. Thomas was not forgotten; he had a large saucer of milk under the tiger lilies.

One of the things that Sara and Abigail liked best of all was to stand at the edge of the bluff overlooking the sea, to stand just as close to the edge as was perfectly safe, and watch the fishing boats come in. The sea was clear and blue, the beach was a long sandy crescent, and the gulls wheeled and screamed above the water.

Thomas often sat at the edge of the bluff with the children. He had been born on a sailing vessel, which, Miss Letty said, was probably the reason why he was so fond of the sea. The twins thought that his interest might have something to do with the smell of fish that so often came to **them** when the wind blew from the fish houses near the wharf, **but** they were too **polite** to mention this to Miss Letty.

Another pleasant thing about the twins **was that** they were extremely helpful about the house. Abigail was especially interested in cooking, and whenever Miss Letty went into the kitchen Abigail was at her heels. Miss Letty would tie on her big white apron and Abigail would tie on hers. Miss Letty would get down the big blue mixing bowl and Abigail was always ready to beat the eggs and sift the flour. Soon she could make cookies that were almost as good as Miss Letty's.

Sara and Abigail at the edge of the bluff, overlooking the sea.

On a rainy day Miss Letty would find Abigail sitting by the kitchen window turning the pages of the big cook book and murmuring dreamily to herself, "Molasses cookies—Aunt Deborah's spice cake—Apple Betty—blueberry muffins—Scotch fancies—Brambles——"

"She is a child after my own heart," said Miss Letty.

Now it is not to be supposed that while Abigail was busy Sara was idle. Sara was especially interested in gardening, and whenever Miss Letty went out into the garden Sara was at her heels. Together they raked and dug and sowed and weeded. Soon Sara knew almost as much about gardening as Miss Letty.

On rainy days Miss Letty often found Sara in a chair by the living-room window looking out at the garden or turning the pages of a seed catalogue and murmuring dreamily, "Nasturtiums—clove pinks—marigolds and lobelia—asters and Shasta daisies—snapdragon and tiger lilies——"

"She is a child after my own heart," said Miss Letty.

If Abigail and Sara had been content with the cook book and the seed catalogue all would have gone well in the little house among the fir trees. Unfortunately they were also very much charmed by a catalogue from Runciman's, a large fat catalogue which told about all the beautiful things that might be ordered from Runciman's for just a little—oh, so little—money.

As the winter evenings went on the twins spent more and more time lying flat on the rug in front of the fire, with the Runciman catalogue spread out before them.

"Oh, look, Miss Letty—such a pretty blue coat with a squirrel

Abigail was especially interested in cooking.

collar! And the pockets are just the kind we both like best of all!"

"And, Miss Letty, see this———"

"We need new linoleum for the kitchen floor———"

"New frilly curtains for our rooms———"

"Warm pink and blue slippers!"

"A red leather collar for Thomas!"

So it went, on and on and on. At last even Miss Letty grew interested in the gay pictures in Runciman's catalogue, and when she found Thomas asleep with both his paws resting on the book she knew it was hopeless. Then the first order was sent. It was for a red leather collar for Thomas. This first package was most exciting, and soon more orders went to Runciman's.

Winter was coming near. The packages from Runciman's began to contain coats and sweaters and galoshes as well as many things that were much more interesting. The days grew shorter and colder.

More and more packages arrived. At least twice a week Abigail and Sara went down the road to the post office by the cove, and came away laden with big and little packages of every size and shape.

The village children watched with wide eyes, wondering whatever could be in the packages. Abigail and Sara could scarcely wait until they reached the cottage to open them. How long the road seemed!

One morning when the twins awoke, the ground was covered with snow. All day long it snowed, so hard and fast that there was nothing but whiteness to be seen. The wind howled and moaned, then it gave loud, fierce shrieks. The windows rattled and the little house on the hill trembled.

"This is one of the worst storms I have known," said Miss Letty. "Strange things must be happening down at the wharf."

"Do you suppose the house will blow away?" asked Abigail.

"No indeed," said Miss Letty, "it has weathered many a storm."

At bedtime the blizzard was still raging. Abigail and Sara shivered as they crept into bed and drew the bedclothes closely around them. For a time they lay and trembled as they listened to the wind in the firs, but it was not very long before they fell asleep.

In the morning everything was calm and quiet. The sky was clear and blue and the sun was shining. The fir trees bent their branches to the ground, and, as Miss Letty said, one could almost hear them complaining about the weight of the snow. The snow lay in great drifts and the lilac hedge in front of the house had completely disappeared. The twins and Miss Letty put on rubber boots and went out into the white world to dig a path to the gate. The snow was hard and crusty and Abigail walked right over the top of the lilac hedge!

Down to the beach they went and found it was a sad-looking place. It was strewn with driftwood and seaweed, and with wreckage of two fishing boats. In the middle of the wharf was a gaping hole, for the fury of the storm had torn loose the heavy piles and boards, and washed them up on the beach. It was so cold that Abigail and Sara were glad to get back to their own warm fireside with Thomas purring on the hearth rug.

In a few days the snow began to melt. Then little rivulets of icy water crept under the shingles of the roof, and in many places inside the house there was a steady drip-drip-drip. Then Miss Letty realized that the roof needed to be reshingled, that there were many necessary things to be bought, and that there was no money in the bank! Miss Letty was not practical.

"It's all the fault of the Runciman catalogue!" said Miss Letty.

"It's all our fault for wanting so many things," said Abigail. "Let's think what can be done." Miss Letty, Abigail, and Sara sat in front of the fire and thought deeply. There was silence for a long time and the only sounds were the steady tick-tick of the big clock on the wall and the contented purr of Thomas.

"I know!" said Abigail suddenly. "Patchwork quilts! People love to buy them and you make such nice ones, Miss Letty. Patchwork quilts for Miss Letty, cookies for me, and—Sara—what will you do? You don't cook, but can't you think of something?"

"I'll go down to the farm and ask if they want a good, strong, helpful girl," said Sara. "But that will be in the spring."

So the patchwork quilts were started and in the winter evenings Miss Letty sat by the fire, sewing squares together, while the twins sat on little stools and joined patches. Abigail and Sara liked the names of the quilt patterns as much as they liked the names in the cook book and the seed catalogue. It was fun to help Miss Letty choose the next pattern to be used: Wedding Ring, Cherokee Rose, Round-about, Wind-Blown Square, Broken Dishes, Give-and-Get. The quilts grew under Miss Letty's skillful fingers and each one seemed more attractive than the one before it.

Abigail and Sara liked the quilting parties, when the big quilting frame filled the little living room, and the neighbors came in and sat quilting, two to a side, tongues going as fast as needles. The twins sat and listened to all the stories that were told, stories of wrecks on the coast, of a mysterious man left stranded on the beach by a passing ship, of Collie the hermit who continued to sit by his fire quite calmly when his roof blew off in the storm. Abigail and Sara wished the neighbors would tell stories all the time instead of talking, as they quite often did, about Mrs. Smith's baby's croup, Aunt Mary's new stove, and Mrs. Hoskin's rheumatism.

When summer came, and with it summer visitors, the quilts were ready! Wedding Ring, Cherokee Rose, Round-about, Broken Dishes—all of them. There were hooked rugs, too. All Miss Letty's hooked rugs had pictures of ships on them, because her father had been a sea captain. There was just one rug that could not be sold, because Thomas had taken it for his own. There he would lie, right in the middle of blue sea and sails, refusing to sleep in any other place. "That is because he was born on the sea," said Miss Letty, indulgently.

Abigail and Sara were busy all summer. Abigail spent mornings in the kitchen and I cannot tell you how many of her crisp brown cookies were eaten by summer visitors. Abigail was glad that the sea air gave them such good appetites.

Sara was most useful on the farm. The farmer just down the road had laughed when Sara asked him if he wanted a good, strong, useful girl, but he soon stopped laughing and said that she was "worth her weight in gold." Sara brought the ducks up from the pond, fed the chickens, and took care of the garden. The farmer's wife said she wondered how she had ever managed without her.

As for the Runciman catalogue, Sara and Abigail had hidden that among the quilts in the chest under the stairs. "It can stay there until we truly need it," they said.

So, with quilts and rugs, cookies and ducks, soon there was a nice sum of money in the bank.

The green, sunny fields looked very peaceful as Miss Letty and the twins walked to church on Sunday mornings. Miss Letty, Abigail and Sara felt peaceful, too, for the roof was newly shingled, the doors and windows freshly painted, and everything was snug and comfortable in the little cottage among the fir trees.

THE SEVEN WHITE CATS

THE SEVEN WHITE CATS

The seven white cats lived on a farm in Sandy Cove. It was a pleasant farm, halfway between the blue waters of the Bay of Fundy and the smiling waters of Saint Mary's Bay.

No one believed in the seven white cats until he had seen them. "Seven white cats? Ridiculous and absurd." That was what everyone said. But there were the cats, plainly to be seen if one took the trouble to walk up the hill to the farmhouse. Often Miranda, the farmer's little girl, would be sitting on the steps with all the cats around her.

It was Miranda who had given them their names. The mother of them all was Blue Eyes. The two half-grown kittens were the Angel Cat and the Odd Cat. The Angel Cat was a beautiful pure white with large blue eyes like her mother's; the Odd Cat was a trifle scrubby looking, and his eyes did not match, for one was blue and one was yellowish brown. Then there were the four smallest kittens, little balls of white fur, always tumbling over each other in the grass or chasing each other's tails. Three of them were Tim, Tip, and Tinker. The fourth was called Stub, because he had only a stub of a tail. The kittens had been brought up in the barn and, sad to relate, Stub's tail had been stepped on by one of the oxen!

Miranda was particularly fond of cats. Her father, Mr. Saunders, was not at all fond of cats, but he was fond of Miranda and so he allowed her to keep them. At least, he allowed her to keep them until one terrible day when everything went wrong. That day was indeed an unlucky one for the seven cats.

The trouble began almost before dawn, when Mr. Saunders went out to milk the cows. Stub, in spite of his accident, was always in the barn, and he ran right in front of Mr. Saunders, who tripped over him and dropped the milk pail. This made Mr. Saunders very angry.

Things kept on happening all through the day. When Mrs. Saunders went into the dairy, she found Blue Eyes helping herself to the biggest bowl of cream. Like other white cats with blue eyes, this cat was deaf, and she did not hear Mrs. Saunders coming. A little later in the day Tinker climbed up the lace curtains in the living room, and tore a large hole in one of them. Tip tangled himself up in Mrs. Saunders' knitting and Tim played havoc with her workbasket.

"Cats are a nuisance!" said Mrs. Saunders.

"There are not going to be any cats on this farm," said Mr. Saunders.

"Oh, please, Papa!" said Miranda.

Mr. Saunders did not pay any attention to Miranda. When he made up his mind to be firm, he was very firm. That afternoon when Miranda was out visiting one of her friends, he bundled all seven white cats into a large crate, loaded the crate on the ox cart, along with baskets of vegetables, and started off. There was a great scuffling and miaowing. From one side of the crate came a white paw, and from the other two blue eyes looked out beseechingly. Mr. Saunders was very hard-hearted.

First of all he drove up the hill to Miss Letty's house. Her adopted twins, Abigail and Sara, were delighted to have a white kitten. They chose Stub because they liked his funny short tail.

Then Mr. Saunders drove down the hill. There seemed to be only one place where he could leave the Angel Cat, that was at the parsonage. As luck would have it, there was the minister's wife, standing by the gray stone wall pruning her lilac bushes.

"This," said Mr. Saunders, "is the cat you need. Her name is Angel, most suitable for a parsonage cat. You will find her good company when the minister is writing his sermons."

Then Mr. Saunders drove on, leaving the minister's wife looking very much surprised, holding the Angel Cat in her arms.

Now Mr. Saunders was well on the road to Tiverton, a fishing village, where he intended to exchange his vegetables for dried fish. The oxen jogged slowly and steadily along. Mr. Saunders guided them with "Gee!" and "Haw!" and an occasional flick of his whip. He did not hurry them, for no one hurries in that part of the world.

Up the long hill they went, along the road until they came to the first village, which was Mink Cove. At one side of the road was a sturdy, neat house with a long patch of yellow tansy growing outside the gate. "I am quite sure these folks need a cat," said Mr. Saunders, and, without stopping the oxen, he picked up Tinker and dropped him into the middle of the tansy patch. The oxen plodded on.

A little farther along the road there was a comfortable farmhouse with a large gray barn. A blue wooden cradle stood under the maple tree at the gate, and the farmer's little boy was helping his mother to tuck the baby into it.

"Such a nice family should have a cat," said Mr. Saunders. "Here is a white kitten, exactly the sort of kitten you would like." He held Tim up, so they could see him.

"We'd like to have a white kitten," said the rosy-cheeked farmer's wife. She came over and took Tim from Mr. Saunders. "Thank you very much. Don't you want him yourself?"

"No," said Mr. Saunders, "one white cat may be a very nice thing to own, but seven white cats—" and he drove on.

As the oxen plodded along the road, Mr. Saunders whistled cheerily, for now there were only three more cats. Soon he came to a cottage which looked different from all the other cottages, for instead of weathered shingles it had a bright red roof. The owner of the cottage had just finished painting it and he was standing with his paint pot and paint brush in his hand, admiring it.

"A house with a bright red roof always looks better if there is a white cat somewhere around," said Mr. Saunders. When the ox cart drove on again the man was holding his paint pot and paint brush in one hand and Tip in the other. He was astonished, for he had always thought he did not care for cats.

The oxen jogged on, and the sea came in sight. This was East Ferry, and in a cottage near the edge of the water lived an old lady who had a great deal of rheumatism. She was sitting by the window looking out at her garden and at the hollyhocks which were as tall as the house. Mr. Saunders jumped down from the cart, carried Blue Eyes over to the window, and dropped her into the old lady's

BAY OF FUNDY
MISS LETTY'S TWINS
THE PARSONAGE
THE HOUSE WITH THE TANSY PATCH
THE COTTAGE WITH THE BRIGHT RED ROOF
THE NICE FAMILY
THE HOUSE WITH THE TALL HOLLYHOCKS
WHARVES AT TIVERTON
MAP OF THE CATS FROM SANDY COVE TO TIVERTON

lap, through the wide-open casement, while he stood outside.

"Here's fine company for you on winter evenings," said he. Then he drove on, leaving the old lady almost out of breath.

There was only one cat left, the Odd Cat, and Mr. Saunders was not at all sure that anyone would care to have a cat with such a strangely assorted pair of eyes. They were ferried across the water to Tiverton, where Mr. Saunders left his vegetables. There he found a fisherman who took the greatest fancy to the Odd Cat.

"Cats with eyes like those are lucky," said the fisherman.

Mr. Saunders sang happily as he turned the heads of his oxen towards home. He sang all the way from East Ferry to Tidville. He hummed all the way from Tidville to Little River. From Little River to Mink Cove he neither sang nor hummed, for he had begun to wonder what Miranda would say. From Mink Cove to Sandy Cove he felt very sad indeed.

When the ox cart stopped in front of his own farmhouse, Mr. Saunders saw Miranda sitting on the steps. Big tears were running down her cheeks and she gave her father a reproachful look. Mr. Saunders did not dare to say anything; he unyoked the oxen and took them into the barn.

Miranda's tears continued to flow. It seemed as if nothing in the world would stop them. While she ate her supper, big tears splashed into her bowl of bread and milk. While she fed the ducks and chickens, tears splashed into the dish of chicken feed. The tears were still trickling when Miranda went to bed, yet she said nothing at all.

"This is more than I can stand!" said Mr. Saunders. "We must do something to make her forget those cats. We certainly must."

"I can't think what possessed you," remarked his wife, shaking her head mournfully.

"I don't know, myself," said Mr. Saunders.

The next morning Mr. Saunders told Miranda that he would take her to the lighthouse. Miranda had always wanted to go to the lighthouse, but she did not even smile. "Yes, Papa," was all she said, in a sad little voice.

It was a gray day. Fog blew in from the Bay of Fundy and almost hid the dark green fir trees. All the way to the lighthouse Miranda looked very sad. Mr. Saunders thought of the seven white cats and wished he had kept just one of them.

They drew near the lighthouse, on its rocky point, and Miranda began to be interested. The lighthouse was very white and neat, the rocks were very black and forbidding. The fog had rolled back over the Bay of Fundy, and sea and sky were blue once more. As they went up the path to the lighthouse a baby came toddling out of the door, a pink and gold baby who laughed and held out her hands to Miranda. Miranda smiled—just a little smile. The lighthouse keeper's wife came out to see that the baby was safe.

And then—a black and white cat came through the doorway. Behind her came four kittens: a black and white kitten, a black kitten, a gray kitten, and—last of all—a white kitten with blue eyes.

Miranda sat right down on the rocky ground and called the kitten. She picked it up and hugged it closely to her. For the first time that day she looked perfectly happy.

"Your little girl seems to be very fond of cats," said the lighthouse keeper's wife.

"She certainly is," answered Mr. Saunders, a trifle grimly.

Miranda sat and held the white kitten.

"Would you like to take my white kitty home with you?" asked the lighthouse keeper's wife.

"Yes! Oh, yes, I would!" answered Miranda. "May I, Papa?"

"I suppose so," sighed her father. "Now let's go and see the light."

Miranda would not let go of the white kitten even for a moment. She was much more interested in the kitten than she was in the funny little winding stairs inside the lighthouse, or in the great revolving light at the top. In fact she wanted to start for home as soon as possible.

As they came up the road to the farmhouse Miranda and Mr. Saunders could scarcely believe their eyes. There, sitting sedately on the doorstep, were Blue Eyes, the Odd Cat, and the Angel Cat. The four kittens scampered around in the grass.

"Why!" said Miranda. "Why, here are all the cats! They must have walked home." She gathered all the cats that she could hold into her arms and hugged them. "I'm so happy!" she said.

Mr. Saunders said nothing at all, but after that there were eight cats at the farmhouse. And all the way from Tiverton to Sandy Cove people said to each other, "Have you seen a white cat anywhere? We had one here the other day."

THE GOLDEN WEDDING

THE GOLDEN WEDDING

Mary and Edward were proud of being the only children in the village who had a great-grandmother and a great-grandfather. Grandmothers and grandfathers were as common as Queen Anne's lace, and grew everywhere, but great-grandparents were something quite different.

Great-grandmother Smith was little and plump and rosy. She wore checked gingham dresses, and spent a good deal of time in the kitchen, making cookies for all the village children.

Great-grandfather Smith was tall and plump and rosy, with lovely white whiskers. He often wore a captain's hat, because he had been a sea captain, and he spent a great deal of time on the porch looking out over Saint Mary's Bay. Sometimes he told stories to Mary and Edward. The stories usually began, "When I was captain of the *Mary Ellen*," and the most remarkable things happened in them.

Great-grandmother and Great-grandfather Smith had been married for fifty years and so they were going to have a golden wedding. There was to be a party to which everyone in the village was invited, and of course everyone would bring a golden present. Mary and Edward heard the most interesting conversations as they stood by the window of the post office waiting for the postmaster to sort the mail.

"I am making a wedding-ring quilt all in gold and lavender," said Miss Letty.

"My grandmother's gold thimble will be just the thing," said Mrs. Saunders.

"I have a gold scarf pin that belonged to my Uncle Daniel," said Zebedee's mother.

Mary and Edward listened and wondered what they could give. They asked Mr. Cossaboom, who kept the village store, but he shook his head.

"I have almost everything you might want," he said. "I have candy, groceries, and rubber boots, besides these neat little canoes that are really pincushions. Unfortunately, the only golden thing I have in the store is oranges. Would oranges do?"

"No!" said Mary and Edward. "Oranges are much too common!"

The day of the golden wedding came nearer and nearer. Mary and Edward were quite unhappy. All the grandchildren would come from Digby, from Annapolis Royal, from Rossway and Tiverton, bringing with them golden presents. What was to be done?

At almost the last moment, a remarkable thing happened. In the middle of the night Miranda Saunders woke up with a terrible toothache. In the early hours of the morning Emma Dakin woke up with a worse toothache than Miranda's.

The next day Miranda's mother talked with Emma's mother, and they decided that Emma and Miranda must go to the dentist in the town across Saint Mary's Bay. Harry would have to take them across in his boat.

Mary and Edward were sorry that Miranda and Emma had the toothache, but they were glad that Harry's boat would be crossing the bay, for it meant that almost everyone in the village would go. It meant that Mary and Edward could buy a golden present in one of the many stores in the town across the water.

On Monday morning, the very day before the golden wedding, everyone hurried down to the wharf and soon the *Lottie Marguerite* was as crowded as a boat could be. Miranda and Emma sat on the deck with their hands to their cheeks, looking quite sad. Mary and Edward tried to be sympathetic but could not help feeling cheerful whenever they thought of the golden present. Mary held a small red leather purse tightly in her hand and every now and then she opened it to see if the money was still there, and it always was.

It was a fine, sunny day with a little breeze blowing. The *Lottie Marguerite* fairly danced across Saint Mary's Bay, her sail as white as the gulls that rocked on the water. It seemed no time at all before the farther shore was reached and the *Lottie Marguerite* safely tied to the pier. Then everyone went ashore.

Mary and Edward looked at the long street with its rows of stores. Which should they try first? In the window of one little store twinkled pins and watches, bracelets and earrings. This seemed to be just the place, so Mary and Edward went in. The kind little man who stood behind the counter peered at them over his spectacles.

"A golden present? Yes indeed!" He brought out a tray full of brooches and bracelets. Mary and Edward looked it over carefully, but everything was too expensive. The most interesting things were not gold, and golden things cost far too much. That was how it went in all the other stores, too. It seemed as if the money in the red leather purse would not buy a present, and Mary and Edward were quite discouraged. Then they came to a queer little shop at the end of the street.

It was a very queer little shop, all hung with hooked rugs and filled to overflowing with strange old teapots, pitchers, and plates. Edward and Mary walked carefully among andirons and ladder-back chairs until they reached the counter. The old lady who kept the shop seemed most amiable.

"A golden present?" she said. "Let me see. Yes, I have the very thing." From the crowded, dusty shelves she took a large plate.

It was a wonderful plate. All around the edge, it was gold and shiny. In the middle there was a picture of a ship with all sails set. It was exactly the sort of plate one would give to a sea captain. It would be an excellent plate for cookies. And it cost two dollars which was exactly the amount in the red leather purse.

"We'll take it!" cried Edward and Mary.

When the *Lottie Marguerite* sailed back across the bay, Mary and Edward sat on the deck looking very happy. They took turns holding the plate which was in a neat brown paper package. The *Lottie Marguerite* danced over the waves as if she knew that she was carrying a beautiful golden present.

The next day was the longest that Mary and Edward had ever spent. The grandchildren arrived from Digby, from Annapolis Royal, from Rossway and Tiverton. They carried packages which looked as if they might contain solid gold presents, and Mary and Edward began to wonder about the plate. The grandchildren were most important. They bustled around and seemed to be doing a great deal. There was nothing that anyone as young as Mary and Edward could do.

At last it was time for the party. Great-grandmother and Great-grandfather sat under an arch of tansy and golden rod made by the grandchildren. Great-grandmother wore her best silk dress and Great-grandfather wore his Sunday suit. The presents were given one by one.

Miss Letty's wedding-ring quilt was, Great-grandmother said, the handsomest she had ever seen. The grandchildren's presents were very gold and very beautiful. When it came time for Mary and Edward to give theirs, they felt most doubtful about the plate. After all, it was only gold around the edge.

Great-grandmother untied the big bow of yellow ribbon, and folded back the tissue paper. The guests and the grandchildren leaned forward to see.

"Well!" said Great-grandmother. "If this isn't exactly what I need! In all this house I couldn't find a plate large enough or handsome enough for the wedding cake."

Great-grandfather looked at the plate. "There's a ship on it, as sure as my name is Jonathan Smith! Now when I was captain of the *Mary Ellen*——"

Great-grandmother and great-grandfather sat under an arch of tansy and golden rod.

Everyone was so busy listening to the tale of the *Mary Ellen* that no one noticed when Mary and Edward disappeared, taking the plate with them. But everyone did notice when, on the last words of the story, Mary and Edward reappeared in the doorway, carrying the cake between them. It was such a grand cake, with its white icing and wedding bells, that it could only have been placed on a golden plate.

The guests and the grandchildren watched as Great-grandmother cut the cake. Mary and Edward almost burst with pride. The presents from Digby and Annapolis, from Rossway and Tiverton, might be very gold and very beautiful but the present from across the bay was the most beautiful and useful of all.

ZEBEDEE, FISHERMAN

ZEBEDEE, FISHERMAN

Zebedee lived in a little house by the Cove. The sea came almost to his front gate.

When he was not in school or asleep, there were two places where Zebedee could be found. One was the old white boat on the beach just below his own cottage. The other was the wharf where the fishing boats came and went. It was on the Bay of Fundy, just half a mile over the hill.

Everyone knew Zebedee because of his wide, cheerful smile and his very blue eyes. They were even bluer than the Bay of Fundy, and that is very blue indeed.

When people first met him they would say, "Zebedee? What a strange name for a little boy!" Zebedee did not mind having a strange name because in the first place everyone called him Zeb, and in the second place his mother had explained to him exactly how he happened to have that name. This is the story:

When Zebedee was born he was the only child in the family, so of course all the aunts and uncles and grandparents wanted to have something to say about his name. The aunts suggested "Earl" and "Everard" and "Leslie." The uncles suggested "John" and "Thomas" and "Richard." The baby's mother did not care for any of these names, nor did the baby's father. There was so much discussion over the naming of this blue-eyed scrap of a baby that when the time came to take him to church to be baptized nothing had been decided. This was very serious. The minister was waiting and there was the baby in his long, white, embroidered christening robe. What was to be done?

"There is only one thing we can do," said Grandfather Harris. He sat down and took the family Bible on his knees. "The first name at which the Book opens shall be the child's."

Grandfather Harris put on his spectacles, opened the Bible, and ran his finger down the page. The aunts and the baby's mother held their breath, hoping the name would not be Ezekiel or Methuselah. Grandfather Harris cleared his throat importantly.

"It is a good name for a fisherman's son, for it was the name of a fisherman," he said. "The name is Zebedee."

Perhaps it was because of his name that Zebedee wished so much to be a fisherman. He loved the sea, he loved boats and fishing lines and rubber boots. He thought there was nothing in the world so interesting and exciting as fishing. It was interesting and exciting all the year round—spring, summer, and autumn.

In the spring it was lobster fishing.

All winter long there was a fence of lobster pots at one side of Zeb's house. In the spring Zeb's father piled all the lobster pots on to an ox cart and jogged slowly up to the Bay of Fundy. Zeb rode on the cart while his father walked beside it. Up the hill they went, past the pond, past Miss Letty's house, and down the steep hill to the wharf. The oxen were so strong and sure-footed they did not seem to mind the heavy load of lobster pots or the rough road.

When the lobster pots were loaded on the boats, Zeb's father and the other fishermen pushed off, leaving him on the wharf.

"Lobster fishing is too cold for little boys," they said.

Zeb went home slowly and sadly.

In the summer Zebedee was almost always on the wharf, but the fishermen would not take him out with them.

"Little boys are a nuisance in boats," they said.

So Zeb watched the boats go out and walked on the wharf among the piles of cod that lay drying in the sun. Sometimes the men would let him help to pile the dried fish into neat little rounded stacks, fish on fish, tail to tail. Zeb loved the smell of the salty, sun-dried cod.

When the fishing boats came in Zeb thought there was nothing more exciting than to help unload the piles of silvery cod and haddock, mackerel and pollock. When the fish were unloaded, Zeb and his father walked home, their rubber boots all covered with glistening scales, their rubber coats smelling beautifully of fish.

On autumn evenings when the moon was full, Zeb was sometimes allowed to stay up late and watch the fishermen drive the herring from Saint Mary's Bay into the Cove. Back and forth on the water darted the fishing boats, each with a great flaming torch at the bow. The herring came straight for the flares and soon the Cove was full of tiny fish, leaping from the water almost into the boats.

Zeb could scarcely stay on the wharf; he longed to have a net and scoop the herring into the boats. The fishermen would not take him out with them.

"It is dangerous for little boys when we have a torch in the boat," they said.

"It's always dangerous for little boys," said Zeb sadly.

At last, when Zeb was seven years old, his father took him fishing. Zeb had to wake up very early. He put on two pairs of stockings, two sweaters, and over the sweaters his rubber coat. Last of all he put on his mittens which were white as a fisherman's mittens must be. It was quite difficult to walk up the hill to the Bay of Fundy in all those clothes. The morning was cold and it was still almost dark. The wind moaned a little in the fir trees. Zeb began to wonder if he really wanted to be a fisherman.

As the boat pushed off from the wharf, Zeb began to feel more cheerful. When they were out in the bay and Zeb's own line slipped through his fingers into the dark, chilly water, he forgot all about the cold and the uncomfortable clothes. When his first fish, a big silver cod, lay in the bottom of the boat there was no happier boy in any fishing village from Sandy Cove to Tiverton.

Now fogs come in suddenly on Fundy, and before the fishermen knew it a thick white fog had blotted out the land. There was no beach to be seen, no bluffs, even the wharf had vanished. Perhaps they were opposite the wharf, perhaps they were nearer the wicked rocks just off the point.

They drifted, waiting for the fog to clear. The boat bobbed up and down on the water, and Zeb began to feel a little queer. His hands were cold, but he said nothing about it. He was sure it was hours before the fog lifted enough for them to see anything. Then the surprising thing was that, after all, they were only a few yards from the end of the wharf! How good the sturdy gray piles looked to Zeb! By the time he had climbed the ladder at the side of the wharf, and started up the hill, he began to feel better, though his head was dizzy and his legs were shaky. In his right hand Zeb carried the big silver cod, in his left hand a large pollock. His rubber boots were covered with glittering fish scales.

At the top of the hill Zeb and his father met Miss Letty's twins coming back from the village.

"Look!" said Zeb, holding up his fish. Abigail and Sara looked, and agreed that they were the finest fish that had ever come out of the Bay of Fundy.

A little farther down the hill, they met Miranda Saunders with a white kitten tucked under her arm. Miranda did not say a word, but Zeb knew that she wished she could go fishing.

When they reached the little house by the Cove, Zeb's mother was at the gate watching for him. A refreshing smell of dinner came through the front door. Zeb's mother admired the cod and the pollock.

"Weren't you afraid, out there in the fog?" she asked.

"No!" said Zebedee.

"Weren't you cold?"

"Not a bit!" said Zebedee, though his hands were blue.

"Or seasick?"

"Of course not"—although the ground on which he stood had a curious way of coming up to meet him.

There was not the least doubt that Zebedee was a fisherman!

WHITE CHRISTMAS

WHITE CHRISTMAS

MARYLEE MARIE lived in the neatest farmhouse on the shore of Saint Mary's Bay. The house was very white and green with tall pink geraniums looking out of every window. The wood pile was the longest and most carefully stacked of all the wood piles from Digby to Tiverton and even the rosy apples on the trees looked as if they had just been scrubbed.

In the summertime, Marylee Marie liked to feed the chickens, to bring the cows home from pasture, and to ride, perched high on her father's blue hay wagon. In the winter it was lonely in the farmhouse which stood by itself quite a distance from any village. The only interesting thing that happened on long winter days was the arrival of the mail bus from Digby. When the bus came Marylee Marie would run out to get the mail bag and to talk to Jim, the driver. Everyone liked Jim, for he was always friendly and cheerful, always singing or whistling. Usually his seat in the bus was surrounded by small packages which might be shoes for the young Browns, a kettle for Miss Letty at Sandy Cove, or any sort of strange thing that people asked him to buy for them.

In December just before Marylee Marie's seventh Christmas, the mail bus brought her a letter from her aunt in Boston. The letter said:

"Dear Marylee Marie:

This is the first year you have had electric light in the farmhouse, so I am going to send you some colored lights for your Christmas tree. Some day next week Jim will bring them to you on the bus."

After that Marylee Marie could hardly wait for the days to go by. They seemed to go very slowly. At last it was three days before Christmas—but still the lights had not come. That morning Marylee's father said:

"Marylee Marie, if we are going to have a Christmas tree we must get it to-day. Storm warnings are out, and, with the snow that is already here, it looks as though we'd have a real old-fashioned white Christmas."

So Marylee Marie put on her warm blue coat, her red cap, her scarf and rubber boots, and started out with her father. Although there were trees growing near their own gate they went far up the hill to the pasture, for they were looking for a tree that would be quite perfect in shape. It was very still among the trees. Sometimes a chickadee called "Chick-a-dee-dee-dee!" or a tiny red squirrel chattered at them from a branch overhead. Most of the time the only sound was the crunch of crisp snow under rubber boots.

By the far pasture bars they found the tree, a slim, fragrant balsam. Marylee's father cut it down with his sharp ax, and they turned homewards, carrying the tree between them and walking in the tracks they had made before. Through the kitchen door they carried the tree.

"What a beautiful fir," said Marylee's mother, "all trimmed with icicles already. It seems too bad to have to melt them. Put it here by the stove to thaw out."

The tree lay by the stove for an hour or two, and Marylee mopped up the puddles made by melting icicles. At last even the biggest icicle had thawed, and a delightful Christmas-tree smell filled the warm kitchen. Then the tree was set at the window of the dining room looking out across the wintry water of Saint Mary's Bay.

"If only the lights would come!" said Marylee Marie.

By this time snow was falling fast and the wind was rising. All night long it snowed and by morning the wind had become a gale. It blew the snow against the house with little sharp shrieks of fury as if it were trying to blow right through the sturdy walls. That afternoon the bus did not come from Digby.

"Oh!" said Marylee Marie. "Now the lights won't be here in time for Christmas!" She stood by the window of the front parlor looking out at the road through whirling snowflakes. An ox sled went by, slowly and with difficulty, the oxen holding their heads low, snow caked on their broad sides.

"Oh, dear!" said Marylee Marie.

"Don't fret about the lights," said her mother. "Come and help me pack this box for the McLeans. They won't have much of a Christmas unless we make it for them." Marylee forgot her troubles then and scurried around trying to find something for each of the McLean children; the McLeans had so many children, and so little money. It was hard to find something for everyone but surprising how many things proved to be tucked away in bureau drawers or in the old trunk under the bed. The baby's present came out of the old trunk, it was a red knitted cap that had belonged to Marylee Marie, a nice round cap with a ribbon rosette on each side. There was a small blue wagon for the older baby, red scarves for the four-year-old twins, a boat for Tim who was six, and dolls for Margery and Jean. The dolls also belonged to Marylee Marie and it took quite a long time to get them ready. Marylee scrubbed their faces and combed their hair while her mother washed and ironed their clothes. When the dolls looked clean and respectable there was a present for everyone except twelve-year-old John.

"I think we shall have to give John your father's second-best knife," said Marylee's mother. "I shall put in one of your father's ties for Mr. McLean, and this pretty string of blue beads for Mrs. McLean. Then we can fill the top of the box with candy, nuts, and cookies."

Marylee and her mother wrapped all the gifts in gay papers and tied them with ribbons that had been carefully saved from packages of the year before. Then Marylee put a piece of bright red paper over the top of the box and her mother tied it with stout cord. It was all ready when John McLean came in at the back door, stamping the snow off his boots and wiping it from his eyelashes. He grinned, lifted the box to his shoulder, and tramped off into the snow.

"Tell your mother we'll have a couple of chickens ready for her if she'll send over for them to-morrow," called Marylee's mother.

On Christmas Eve the snow had stopped falling. The sun came out and the steel gray water of Saint Mary's Bay changed to a deep, cold blue. Each fir tree was trimmed for Christmas. The trees and houses cast blue shadows on the snow. Against the farmhouse fence the drifts were deep and rounded like great feather beds, so soft and inviting that Marylee longed to jump into the middle of them. The day went by, slowly, slowly, and at last it was time for the mail. Marylee Marie stood at the gate between two snowdrifts and looked along the white, lonely road. There was the sound of sleigh bells and around the corner came a large sled drawn by two horses. It was the mail, Marylee knew that, for she could hear Jim's familiar, cheerful voice:

"Noel, Noel, Noel, Noel,
   Born is the King of Israel."

The sled stopped by the farmhouse gate, then Jim jumped down and handed a large package to Marylee Marie. She hurried into the house with it, just as her mother came out with a cup of hot cocoa for Jim. Marylee put the package on the floor near the Christmas tree and began to tug excitedly at the string. Soon all the wrappings were removed, and she lifted the cover from a cardboard box. Inside, there were packages of all shapes and sizes. First came two boxes of lights for the tree—Marylee was quite disappointed in those because they looked rather uninteresting. Then there were packages of tinsel and other trimmings—Marylee could scarcely believe her eyes when she saw the white woolly sheep with red ribbons around their necks, the small spotted horses with perky tails, and the gay birds to perch on the tips of the branches. Best of all there was a smiling wax angel with very pink cheeks, gauzy wings, and golden hair—she was for the top of the tree.

"Let's trim it right away!" said Marylee Marie.

It was fun to find places for everything and in a short time the little tree sparkled with tinsel and shone with rainbow-colored trimmings. Then came the great moment when Marylee's father connected the lights. The tree blossomed magically, the tinsel was no longer silver but hung in glittering strands of blue and red and gold. Marylee Marie sat on the floor, looking up at the beautiful thing. There is no telling how long she would have sat there if suppertime and bedtime had not come along. Of course Marylee remembered to hang up a red stocking before she went to bed.

<u>Christmas Day</u> came with packages and a bulging stocking for Marylee Marie. There was the Christmas dinner, with so much duck and plum pudding that afterwards everyone sat very quietly for a long time. Just as it was growing dark there came the sound of bells, not the gay tinkling bells of a horse sleigh but the slow, dignified bells of an ox sled. The sled stopped at the gate and out tumbled six McLean children. They raced to the house, shouting, "Thank you for our Christmas box!" and Mr. McLean followed, carrying the baby. Marylee's mother opened the door, and the whole family filed through the kitchen. They got no farther than the door of the dining room, for there they saw the lighted Christmas tree and stood as if rooted to the floor. For a few minutes no one moved or said a word. Then the fat baby started forward on unsteady legs, holding out one red-mittened hand.

There they saw the lighted Christmas tree.

"Kismus tee!" she said.

After that all the children crowded around the tree and touched the trimmings with timid exploring fingers.

"O-o-oh, look at the baby lambs!"

"Can't I make the green bird sit on another branch?"

"Looky here at Santy Claus!"

"Look at the fairy!"

"Angel," corrected Marylee Marie. She turned the lights on and off several times, so that they twinkled and seemed more wonderful than ever. Then her mother came in with a plate of cookies and the seven McLeans sat around the tree and looked and munched.

When everyone was quite full of cookies, Marylee's mother

called the children over to the parlor organ to sing some Christmas hymns. The little parlor organ was slightly out of tune but that did not matter in the least. The six McLeans sang in shrill clear voices, the twins a little behind the others. When the baby began to grow tired of listening, Mr. McLean tucked her under his arm and bundled the children out-of-doors and into the sled.

Marylee stood at the window and watched them go. "Ding, dong!" went the bells. Star and Bright plodded along, fat and placid, paying no attention to the sled full of wriggling, shouting children. The sled grew smaller in the distance, it turned the corner and was out of sight.

Christmas Day was over. Supper was not important, bedtime was welcome. The little tree stood in the window, its lights twinkling out across the snow. Only the gulls that flew over Saint Mary's Bay could see it, for Marylee Marie was fast asleep under three warm layers of patchwork quilt.

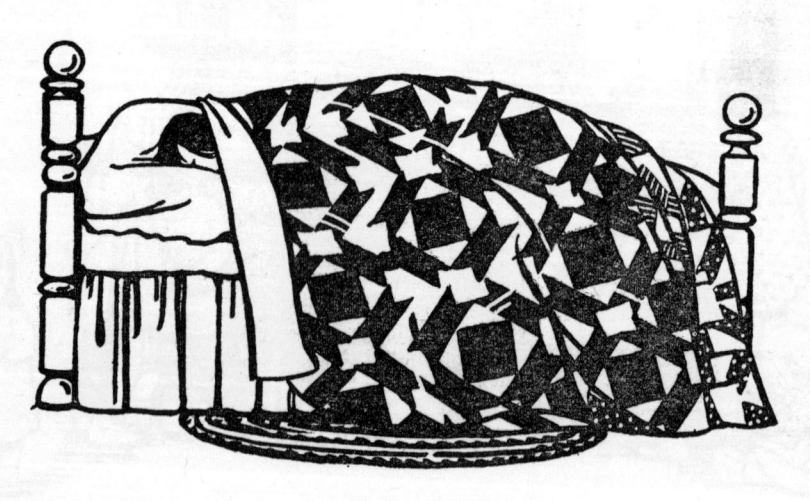